To Clarissa's first friends, the Rovers: Dashka, Brian, and Lissa —M. E.

For Goldie Jo and her folks, with love —S. G.

BLOOMSBURY CHILDREN'S BOOKS
Bloomsbury Publishing Inc., part of Bloomsbury Publishing Plc
1385 Broadway, New York, NY 10018

BLOOMSBURY, BLOOMSBURY CHILDREN'S BOOKS, and the Diana logo are trademarks of Bloomsbury Publishing Plc

First published in the United States of America in July 2020
by Bloomsbury Children's Books

Text copyright © 2020 by Marcus Ewert
Illustrations copyright © 2020 by Susie Ghahremani

Bloomsbury books may be purchased for business or promotional use. For information on bulk purchases please contact Macmillan Corporate and Premium Sales Department at specialmarkets@macmillan.com

Library of Congress Cataloging-in-Publication Data
Names: Ewert, Marcus, author. | Ghahremani, Susie, illustrator.
Title: She wanted to be haunted / by Marcus Ewert ; illustrated by Susie Ghahremani.
Description: [New York] : Bloomsbury Children's Books, 2020.
Summary: Clarissa, an adorable pink cottage, wants nothing more than to be haunted,
but her attempts only make her cuter until she tries being herself and is pleasantly surprised.
Identifiers: LCCN 2019044653 (print) | LCCN 2019044654 (e-book)
ISBN 978-1-68119-791-3 (hardcover) • ISBN 978-1-5476-0385-5 (e-book) • ISBN 978-1-5476-0386-2 (e-PDF)
Subjects: CYAC: Stories in rhyme. | Dwellings—Fiction. | Self-acceptance—Fiction. |
Haunted houses—Fiction.
Classification: LCC PZ8.3.E964 She 2020 (print) | LCC PZ8.3.E964 (ebook) | DDC [E]—dc23
LC record available at https://lccn.loc.gov/2019044653

The artwork was hand painted in gouache, with graphite accents. The artist, Susie Ghahremani, made the choice to paint on black illustration board with the intention that bits of darkness would peek through the brushstrokes, hinting at the "wicked" interior of Clarissa and her world, underneath its cheerful color.
Typeset in Acme, Brandon Grotesque, Burbank, Bubblegum Sans, Kurale, and Zephyr • Book design by John Candell
Printed in China by RR Donnelley, Dongguan City, Guangdong
2 4 6 8 10 9 7 5 3 1

All papers used by Bloomsbury Publishing Plc are natural, recyclable products made from wood grown in well-managed forests. The manufacturing processes conform to the environmental regulations of the country of origin.

To find out more about our authors and books visit www.bloomsbury.com and sign up for our newsletters.

She Wanted to Be HAUNTED

Marcus Ewert

illustrated by
Susie Ghahremani

BLOOMSBURY
CHILDREN'S BOOKS
NEW YORK LONDON OXFORD NEW DELHI SYDNEY

Clarissa was a cottage,
adorable and pink.
Her paint was bright and sparkling,
her windows seemed to wink.
Daisies grew around her,
squirrels scampered on her lawn.
Life was just *delightful!*
            —and it made Clarissa yawn.

See,

her father was a castle,
looming on a crag,
whipped by winds
and cloaked in clouds,
lit just by lightning-jag.

Vampires dwelt within him,
waltzing silently in halls—
bats above,
cold crypts below,
. . . and red stains on the walls.

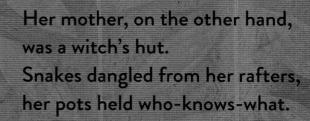

Her mother, on the other hand,
was a witch's hut.
Snakes dangled from her rafters,
her pots held who-knows-what.

Rats and frogs and spells and smells,
an old skull on a shelf—
more creepy than the witch within
was the hut herself!

Buuuuut . . .

Clarissa had a *doorbell*,
and *a* WELCOME *mat*!
Wind chimes tingle-jingled!
(You can't get less cool than that.)

And unlike both her parents,
Clarissa wasn't host
to anybody scary—
            not even one wan ghost!

"I'm lonely!" she admitted.
"I'm lonely, and I'm bored!
I'm just so *ordinary*!
No wonder I'm ignored.

"If only I were *haunted*—
I'd never be alone!
But look at me: I'm *cheerful*!
I've got to change my tone!"

"I've got to look less *friendly*!
I've got to look less *fun*!
I'm sick of all this *daylight* . . .

I've got to block the sun!!!"

She went to see her father,
to ask him for some clouds:

"I need a veil of gloom, Dad,
and shadows that enshroud."

"*Of course* I'll give you clouds, dear!
But may I add advice?
It's *okay* to be yourself—
there's nothing wrong with nice!"

Clarissa thought that over . . .
but left with clouds in tow.
Back at home, she took each cloud
and hung it up just so.

Soon her skies were gray and grim—
a drear, forbidding sight.
Who on earth would feel at home?
A ghost or monster might.

But, oh! Poor Clarissa!
She'd made all her plans in vain!

'Cause what clouds bring us
isn't FRIENDS—
what clouds bring is . . .

RAIN.

Silver strands came streaming down
for seven days or more.
All it did was make Clarissa
cuter than before!

Honeysuckles twined around;
roses grew in bunches;
birds swam in her birdbath
and then shared poolside brunches!

She longed to have her clouds back
    —but they had all dissolved.
She was sadder than before
    —but also, more *resolved*.

She ran to see her mother,
to ask her mom for *stench*—
some smell just one whiff of which
would make one's nostrils clench.

"Mom, I need an odor
that drives living things away!
(How else will I be a house
where ghosts would want to stay?)"

"Of course I'll help you, honey!
But this is what I think:
a true friend likes you 'cause you're YOU,
not because you stink!"

But Clarissa was determined,
and so her mom pitched in.

"Here's a smoking bottle
   that I won once from a djinn.
Unstopper it when you get home
   and out will pour a reek.
Normal kinds of creatures
   will be gone within a week."

Clarissa took the bottle
(forgetting to say thanks).
She raced home excitedly,
a shiver in her planks.

She uncorked the bottle
. . . and soon was wreathed in fumes.
Nasty, noxious vapors
billowed all throughout her rooms.

But nothing *died* nor sped away
(though the grass turned brown).
And who was drawn *toward* the stink . . . ?

All the dogs in town!

They rolled around adorably
(as doggies like to do).
Instead of ghosts, *fur* filled the air
(and lots of slobber, too).

"I give up!" Clarissa cried.
"I'll never get a ghost!
I'm not *remotely* scary—
I'm just 'unkempt,' at most!
Though I've tried to change myself,
I've only made things WORSE.
Flowers, birds, and darling dogs?
It's like some kind of curse!"

The cottage took a deep, deep breath
. . . then she softly sighed.
Could she live a happy life
without a ghost inside?
Could she squash her longing
for a special, spectral friend?

Either way, she knew
her spooky plans had hit an end.

Clarissa took *another* breath
. . . then she loudly said:

"Listen, everybody!
I'm done with the undead!
Since no ghost wants to stay with me,
I'll try something new:
Pretty things can live here now—
including all of you."

"Hooray, hooray, Clarissa!"
the gathered creatures cheered.

But through that throng,
from the back,
a pathway slowly cleared.

Down that path a pony paced
with golden hooves and horn.

All the sunlight shone upon
a snow-white

UNICORN.

I invited prettiness,
Clarissa sadly thought.
So I guess that's pretty much
exactly what I got.

But sometimes life has funny plans
that we cannot predict.
The unicorn was *vicious*—
he bit and spat and kicked.

He chewed up all the flowers,
and then tore up the lawn.
He ran at creatures with his horn
till they all were gone.

Clarissa's never bored now:
her best friend is a brute!
And she can be herself at last:
horrible

        . . . and cute.